D1049889

WITHDRAWN
FROM THE RECORDS OF THE
MID-CONTINENT PUBLIC LIBRARY

RICKY RICOTTA'S MIGHTY ROBOT VS. THE MECHA-MONKEYS FROM MARS

STORY BY
DAV PILKEY

ART BY
DAN SANTAT

SCHOLASTIC INC.

FOR LEWIS AND LUCY BROCK
– D.P.

FOR LEAH
– D.S.

Text copyright © 2002, 2014 by Dav Pilkey
www.pilkey.com

Illustrations copyright © 2014 by Dan Santat
www.dantat.com

All rights reserved. Published by Scholastic Inc. SCHOLASTIC and associated logos are trademarks and/or registered trademarks of Scholastic Inc.

No part of this publication may be reproduced, stored in a retrieval system, or transmitted in any form or by any means, electronic, mechanical, photocopying, recording, or otherwise, without written permission of the publisher.

For information regarding permission, write to Scholastic Inc., Attention: Permissions Department, 557 Broadway, New York, NY 10012.

Library of Congress Cataloging-in-Publication Data

Pilkey, Dav, 1966 – author.
Ricky Ricotta's mighty robot vs. the mecha-monkeys from Mars /
story by Dav Pilkey ; art by Dan Santat. — Revised edition.
pages cm
Summary: A small mouse and his best friend, a giant flying robot, attempt to save the Earth when an evil Martian monkey and his mechanical creations attack.
1. Ricotta, Ricky (Fictitious character) — Juvenile fiction. 2. Mice — Juvenile fiction. 3. Robots — Juvenile fiction. 4. Heroes — Juvenile fiction. 5. Monkeys — Juvenile fiction. 6. Mars (Planet) — Juvenile fiction. [1. Mice — Fiction. 2. Robots — Fiction. 3. Heroes — Fiction. 4. Humorous stories.] I. Santat, Dan, illustrator. II. Title. III. Title: Ricky Ricotta's mighty robot versus the mecha-monkeys from Mars.
PZ7.P63123Row 2014 813.54 — dc23 2014003713

ISBN 978-0-545-63115-0

10 9 8 7 6 5 4 3 2 1 14 15 16 17 18 19

Printed in the U.S.A. 88

Revised edition
First printing, July 2014

Book design by Phil Falco

CHAPTERS

1. The Big Mistake
5

2. Big Trouble
18

3. Major Monkey Hates Mars
22

4. The Trap
29

5. Betrayed
37

6. Major Monkey Makes His Move
47

7. The Mouse from SASA
56

8. The Space Shuttle
61

9. Ricky to the Rescue
80

10. Freedom
87

11. Back to Earth
94

12. The Big Battle (in Flip-O-Rama™)
105

13. Paying for Mistakes
128

14. Heroes
135

CHAPTER ONE
THE BIG MISTAKE

One day, Ricky Ricotta and his Mighty Robot were playing hide-and-seek in their yard.

"This game is too easy," said Ricky. "Let's ride skateboards instead!"

Ricky got his skateboard out of the garage, but there was no skateboard big enough for his Mighty Robot.

"I know," said Ricky. "We can use my parents' minivan!"

Soon, Ricky and his Mighty Robot were zooming down the street.

"This is fun!" said Ricky.

But it stopped being
fun when they wiped out.

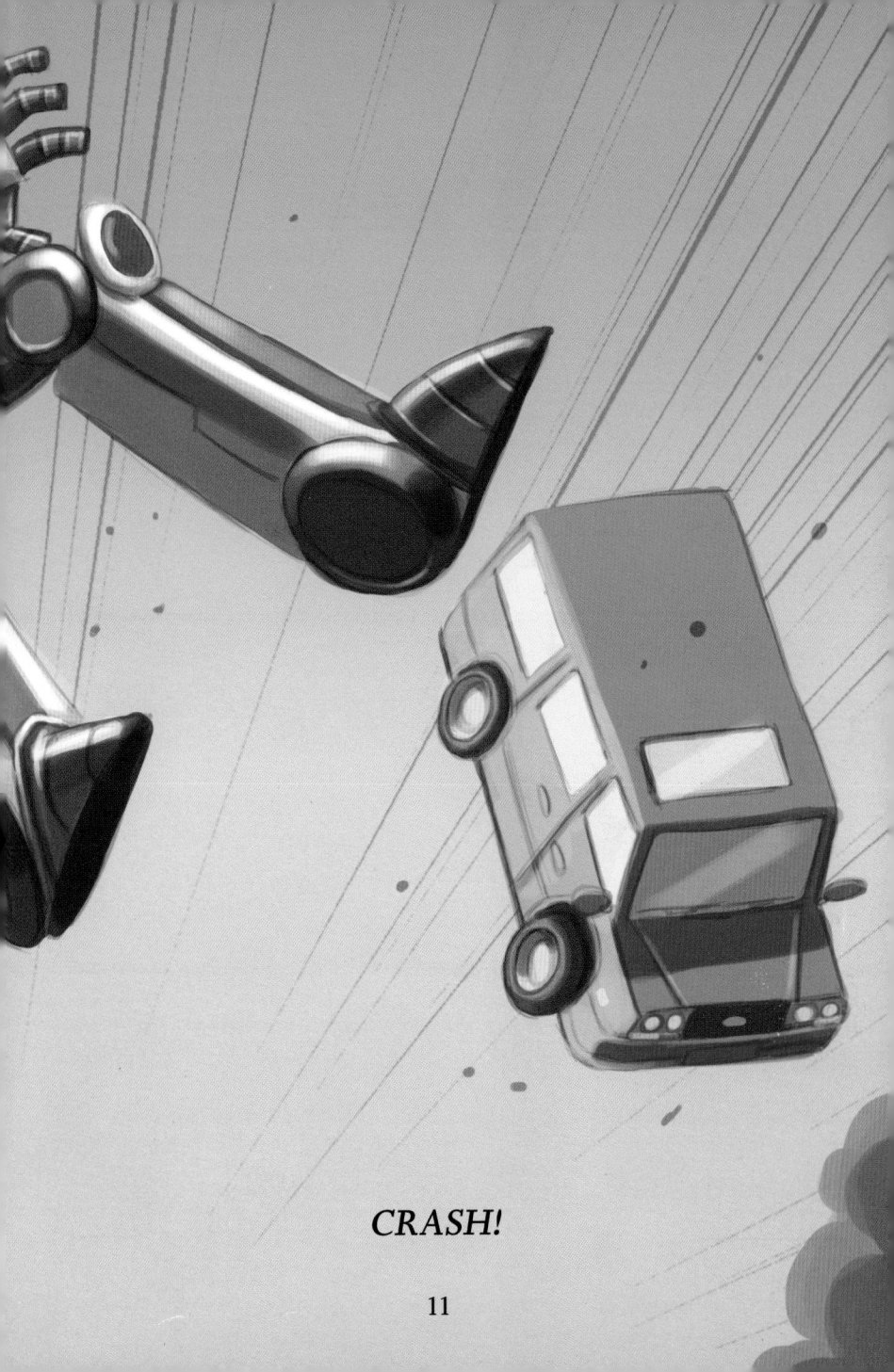

CRASH!

SPLASH!!!

When Ricky and his Robot got out of the pond, they saw the smashed-up minivan.

"Uh-oh," said Ricky. "We're in big trouble now!"

Ricky's Mighty Robot put the minivan back in the driveway.

"Maybe Mom and Dad won't notice," said Ricky.

But they did.

CHAPTER TWO
BIG TROUBLE

Ricky's mother and father were not happy.

"All right," said Ricky's father. "Which one of you boys squished our minivan?"

Ricky and his Mighty Robot looked down at the ground. They were very worried.

Finally, Ricky confessed.

"We both did," said Ricky. "It was an accident."

"You boys were very irresponsible," said Ricky's father.

"Yes," said Ricky's mother, "and you will have to find a way to pay for the damage you have done."

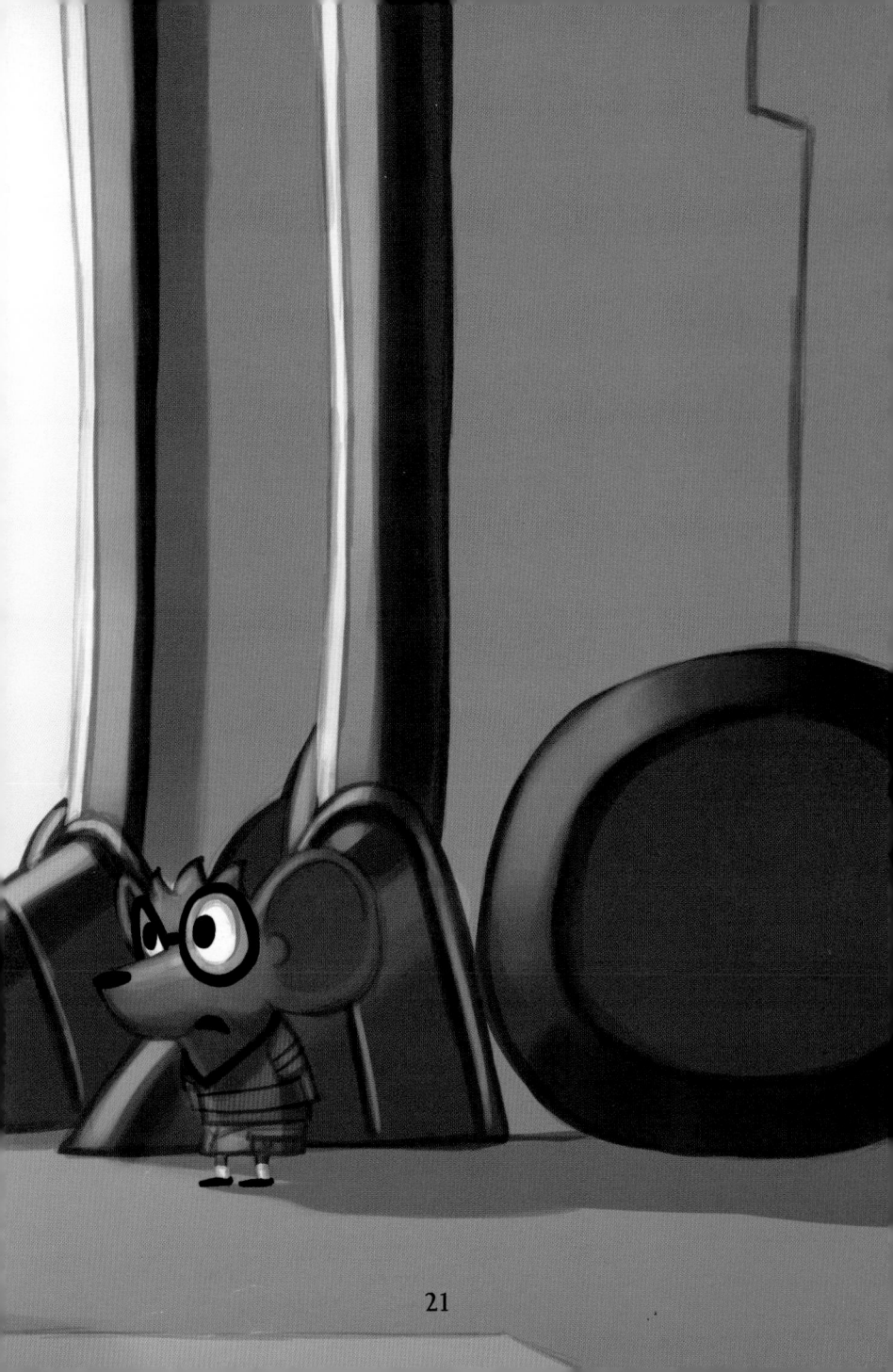

CHAPTER THREE
MAJOR MONKEY HATES MARS

Meanwhile, about 35 million miles away, on the planet Mars, there lived a mean little monkey who was hatching an evil plan.

His name was Major Monkey, and he hated living on Mars. Mars was a cold, dry, and very, very lonely place.

Major Monkey kept himself busy by building evil robots and strange machines in his secret laboratory, but he was still lonely.

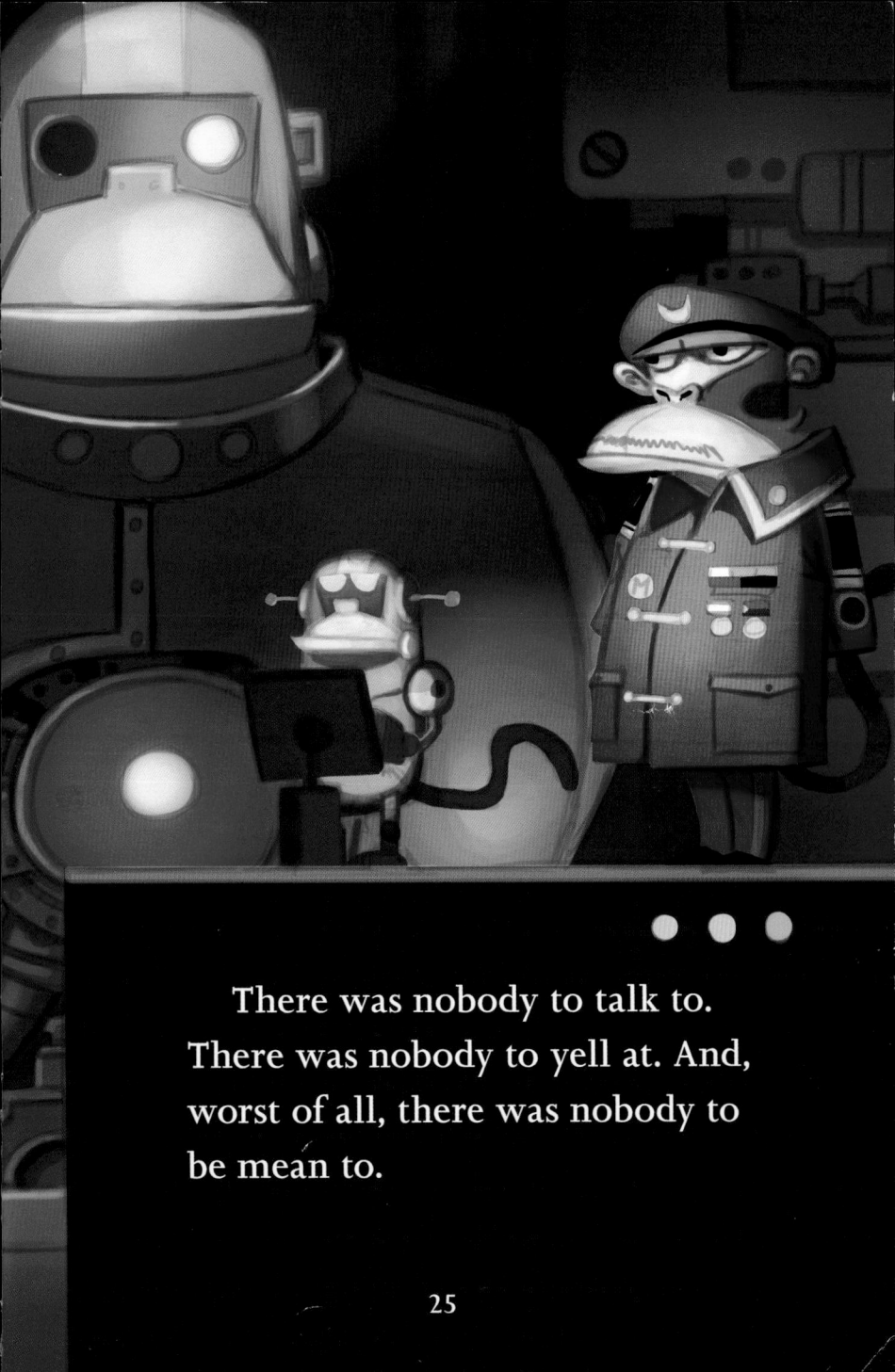

There was nobody to talk to. There was nobody to yell at. And, worst of all, there was nobody to be mean to.

So Major Monkey decided to take over the planet Earth and enslave all of mousekind.

Major Monkey had watched Earth for many months. He saw other evil villains try to take over the planet, but they were always stopped by Ricky Ricotta's Mighty Robot.

"I must get rid of that Mighty Robot!" said Major Monkey. "And I know just how to do it."

CHAPTER FOUR
THE TRAP

The next morning, as Ricky and his Mighty Robot walked to school, they tried to think of a way to pay for their mistake of wrecking the minivan.

"How many years will it take to buy a new minivan with my allowance?" asked Ricky.

Ricky's Robot used his super brain to figure out the answer.

"Hmmm," said Ricky. "Only 259 years? Maybe we should think of a better plan."

Suddenly, a small spaceship zoomed out of the sky. The top of the spaceship opened up, and a spacemouse peeked out.

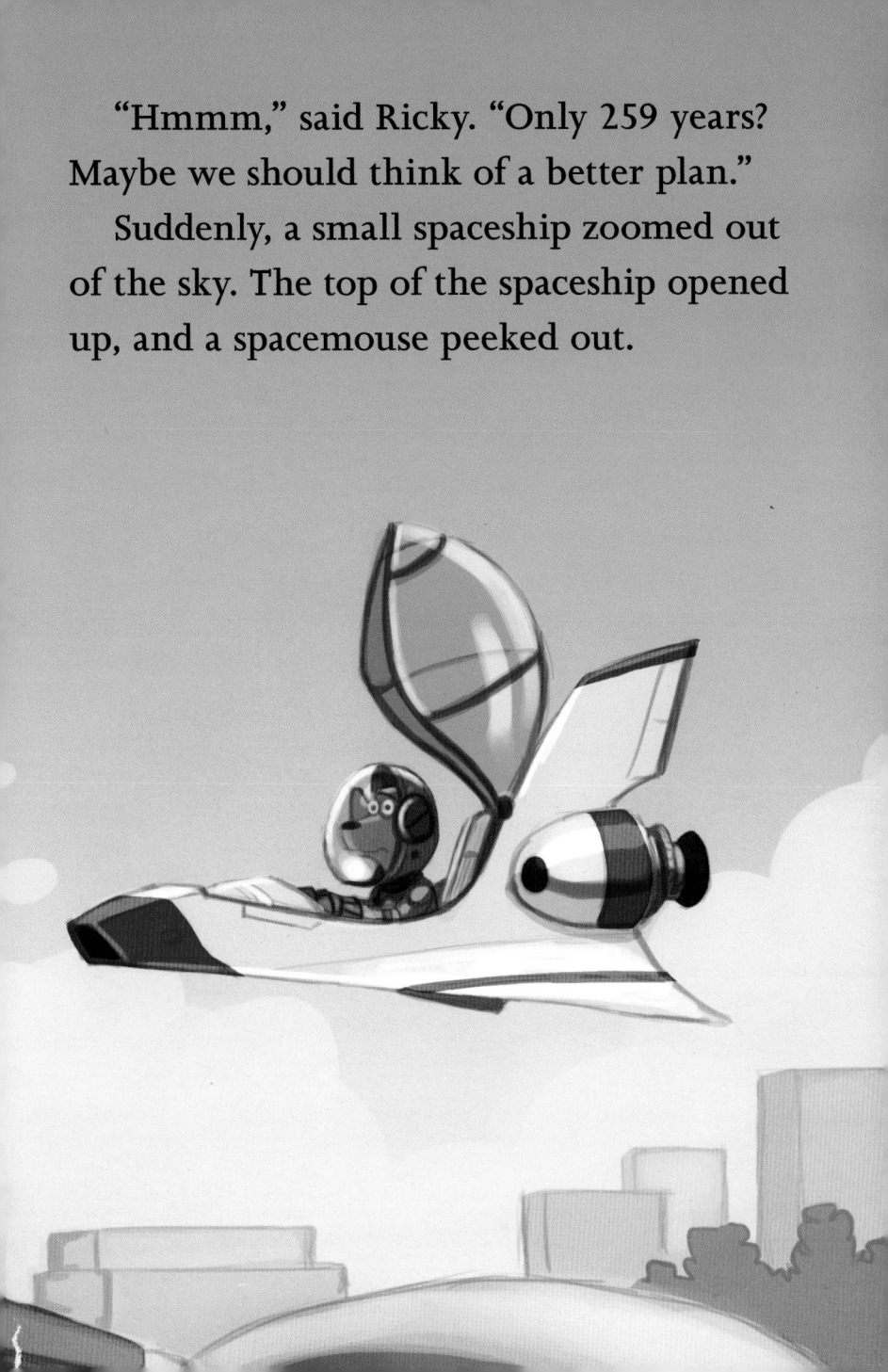

"Help us! Help us!" cried the spacemouse. "Mars is under attack! We need your Mighty Robot to save us!"

Ricky Ricotta's Mighty Robot could not turn away from someone who needed help. So the Mighty Robot followed the tiny spaceship all the way to Mars.

"Be careful up there!" Ricky shouted.

CHAPTER FIVE
BETRAYED

Ricky's Mighty Robot soon arrived on Mars. He saw a strange laboratory, but he did not see any evil villains.

The Mighty Robot flew closer to the laboratory. Suddenly, a giant metal hand reached out of the hillside.

It grabbed Ricky's Robot and would not let go.

Ricky's Mighty Robot tried and tried, but he could not escape the grip of the giant metal hand.

Major Monkey looked up from the spaceship and pulled a mask off his head.

"I tricked you! I tricked you!" Major Monkey mocked. "Now it is *YOU* who needs help! Haw-haw-haw!"

Major Monkey pressed a button inside his spaceship. Soon, three giant Mecha-Monkeys rose from the depths of the strange laboratory.

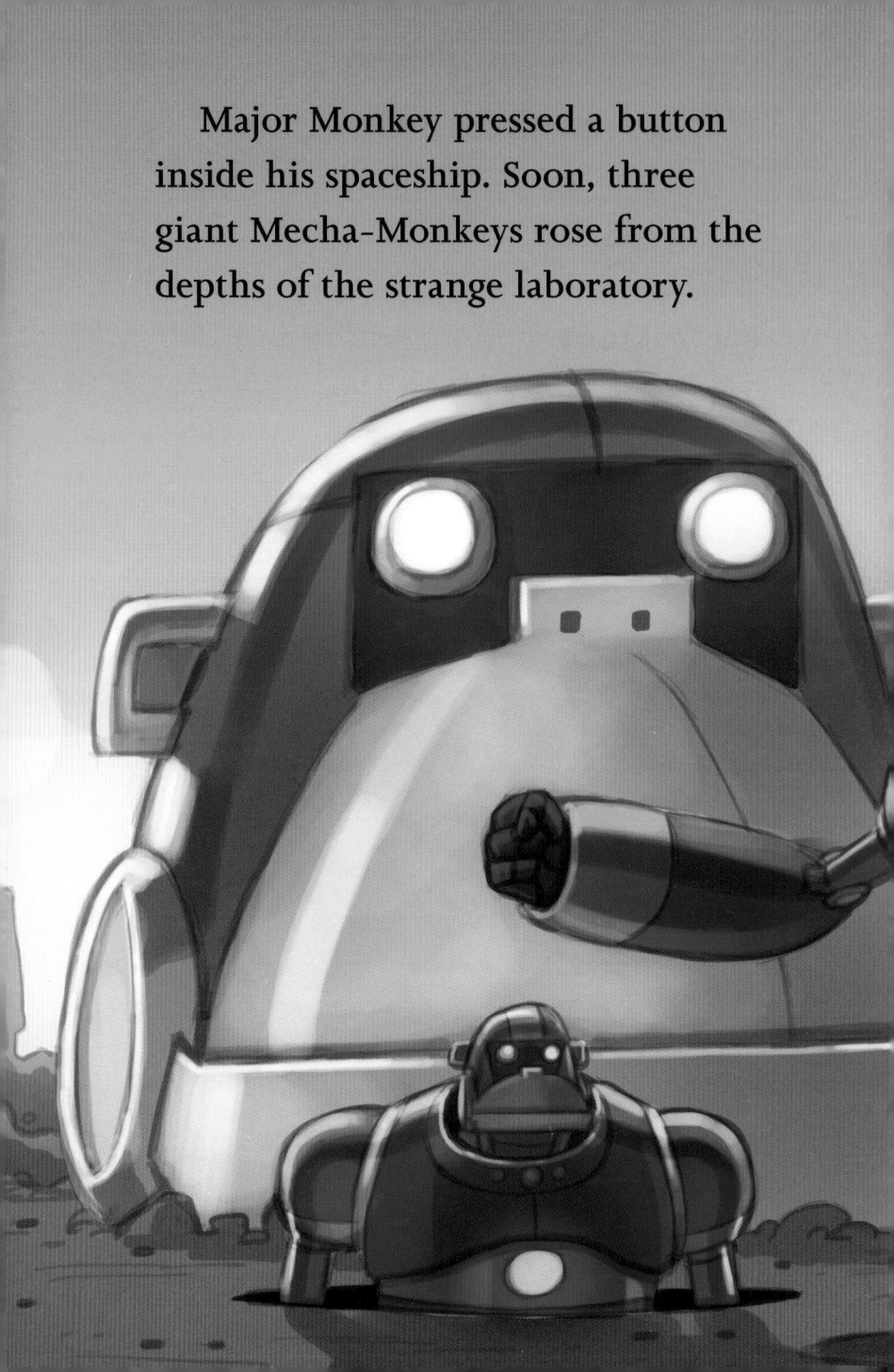

Major Monkey called out to his troops. "Mecha-Monkeys!" he cried. "It is time to take over Earth. Follow ME!"

CHAPTER SIX
MAJOR MONKEY MAKES HIS MOVE

Ricky was taking a spelling test when he saw the little spaceship return with three enormous Mecha-Monkeys.

"Hey," cried Ricky, "where's my Robot?"

"He got into a tight squeeze," laughed Major Monkey. "And he's never coming BACK — haw-haw-haw!"

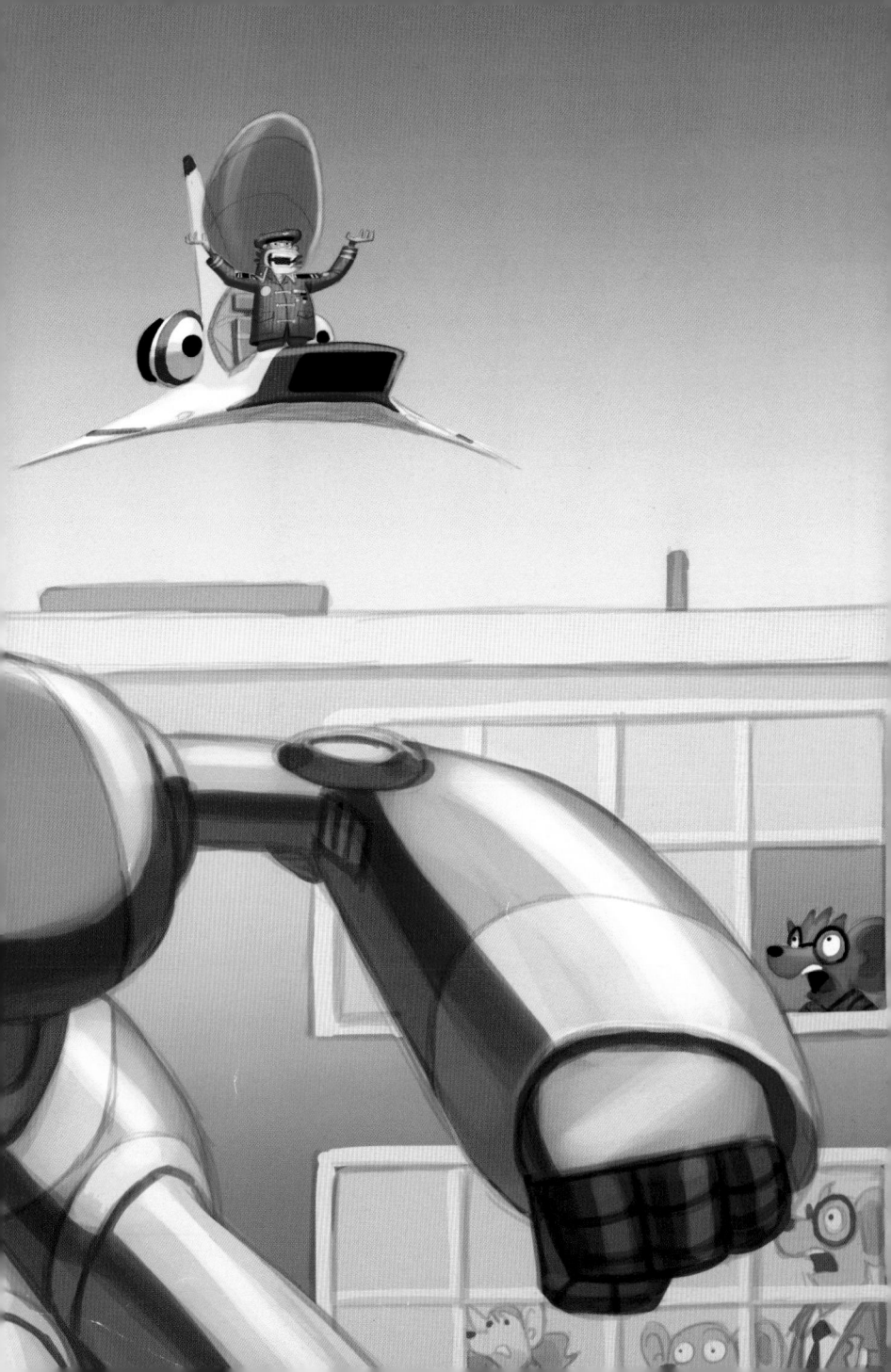

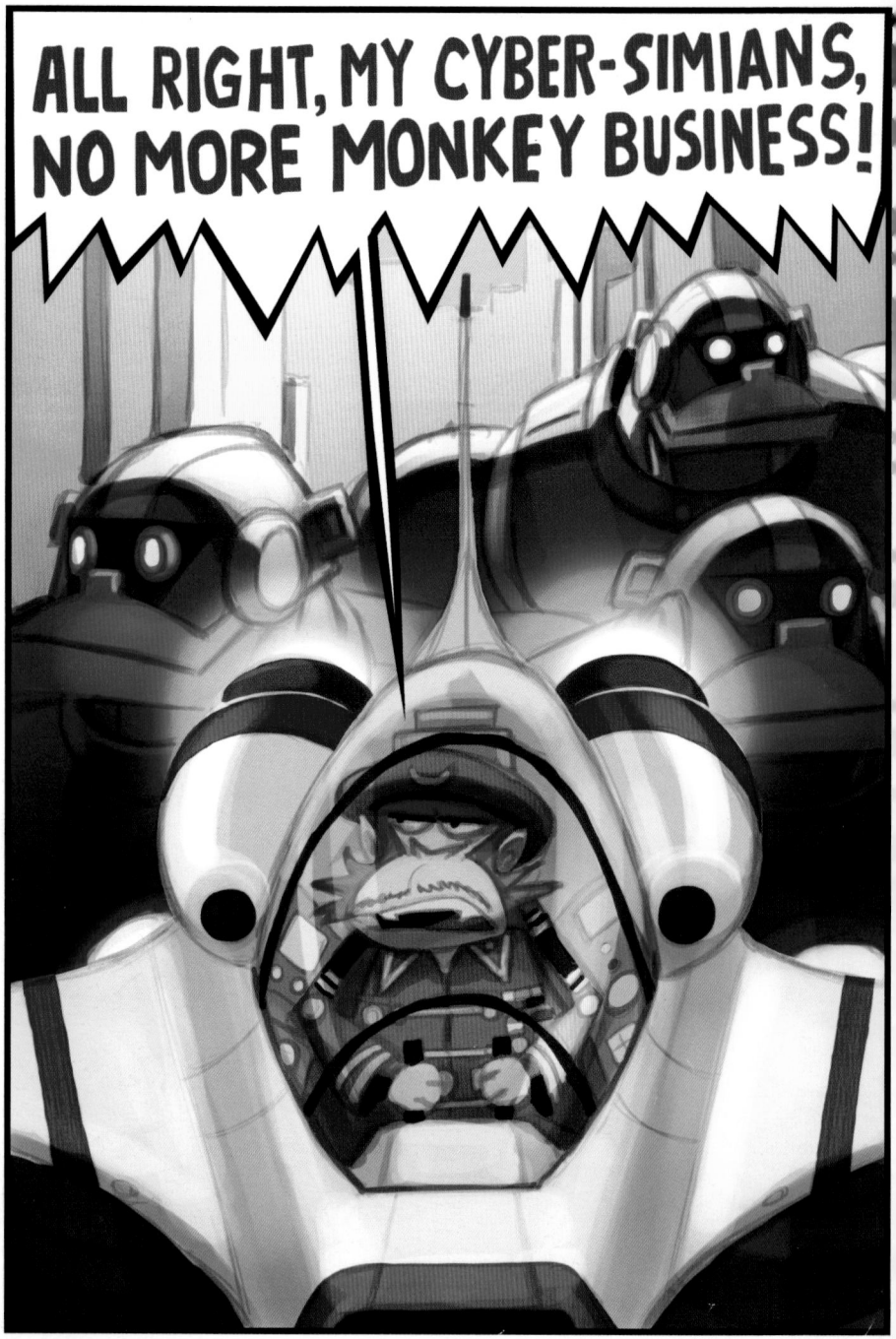
ALL RIGHT, MY CYBER-SIMIANS, NO MORE MONKEY BUSINESS!

ATTACK!!
ICE
KA-BOOF

NOOOO!!
KEEP GOING!
BOOM

SHOOOOOOOOOOOOOOOF
KER-SMASH!

HAW! HAW! HAW! HAW!

THE EARTH IS MINE!!
AND NOBODY CAN STOP ME NOW!

CHAPTER SEVEN
THE MOUSE FROM SASA

Things were not looking good for Earth.

"If only my Mighty Robot were here," said Ricky. "He'd stop those crazy monkeys and save us all."

"Don't worry," said Ricky's father. "I'm sure he'll find a way to escape."

Soon, there was a knock on the front door. It was a general from the Squeakyville Air and Space Association.

"We are going to send a space shuttle up to Mars to rescue your Mighty Robot," said the general. "He is our only hope."

"Hooray!" cried Ricky.

"And we need you to come with us, Ricky," said the general. "You know that Robot better than anybody."

"Can I go?" Ricky asked his parents. *"Pleeeeeease?"*

"Well," said Ricky's father, "all right. But you must promise to be careful!"

"Hooray!" cried Ricky.

CHAPTER EIGHT
THE SPACE SHUTTLE

Ricky and his parents got into the general's car. The general turned on the rocket boosters, and they all flew straight to the Space Center.

"This is *so cool*!" said Ricky's father.

Soon, Ricky was sitting inside a giant space shuttle with three real astromice.

Ricky fastened his seat belt, and off they blasted into outer space.

When the shuttle arrived on Mars, Ricky and the astromice saw Major Monkey's laboratory.

They saw the Mighty Robot trapped inside the giant metal hand. But what could they do?

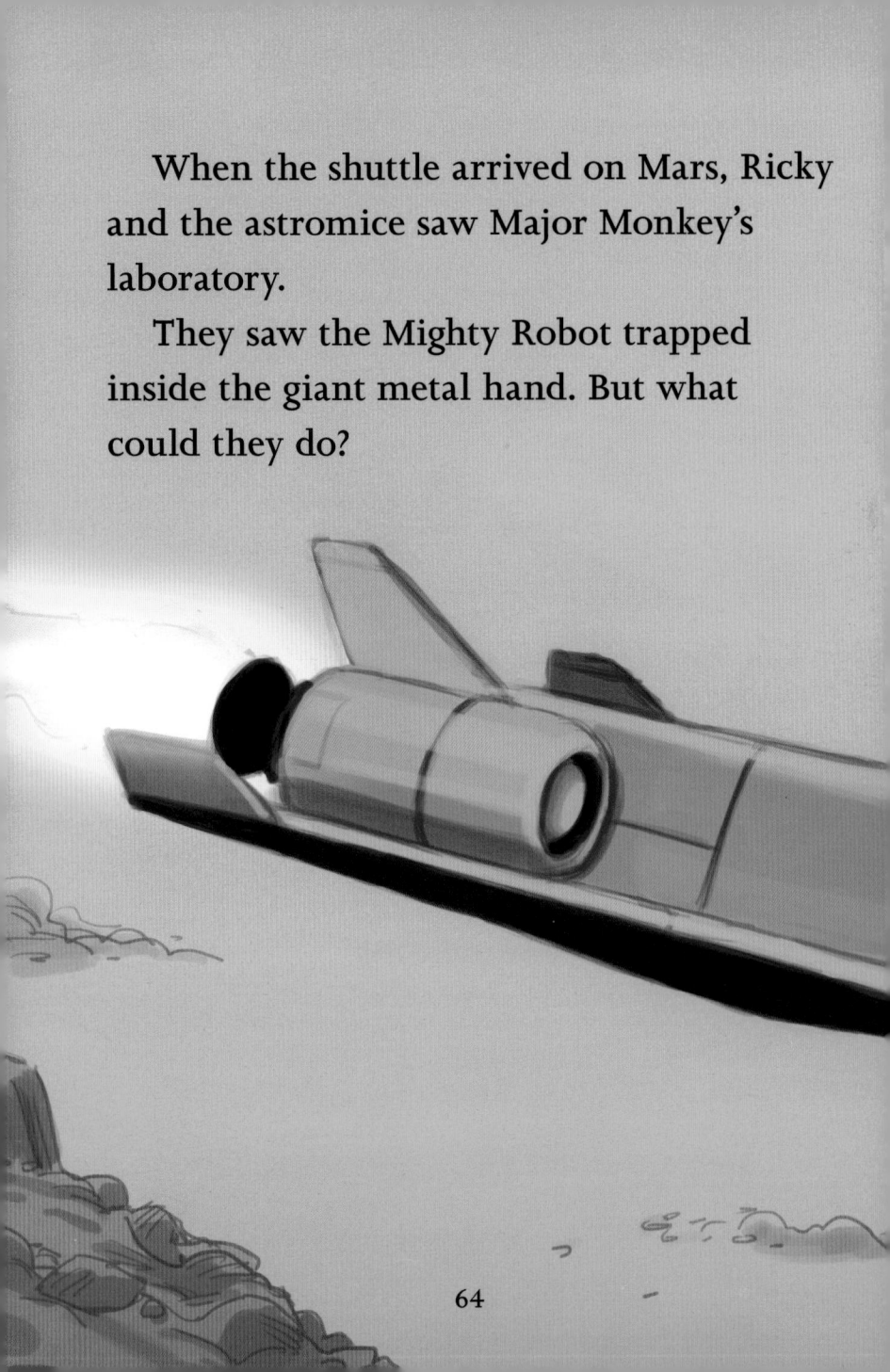

Suddenly, another giant metal hand reached out of the hillside and grabbed the space shuttle.

Then the strange laboratory began to rise from the ground.

It rose higher and higher . . .

. . . until finally it stepped out of the ground. Major Monkey's laboratory had turned into a colossal Orangu-Tron.

The astromice inside the space shuttle tried to open the emergency exit door, but it was stuck.

OH NO! THE ESCAPE DOOR WON'T OPEN ALL THE WAY!
EMERGENCY EXIT DOOR
MAYBE I CAN SQUEEZE THROUGH!
ALMOST THERE...

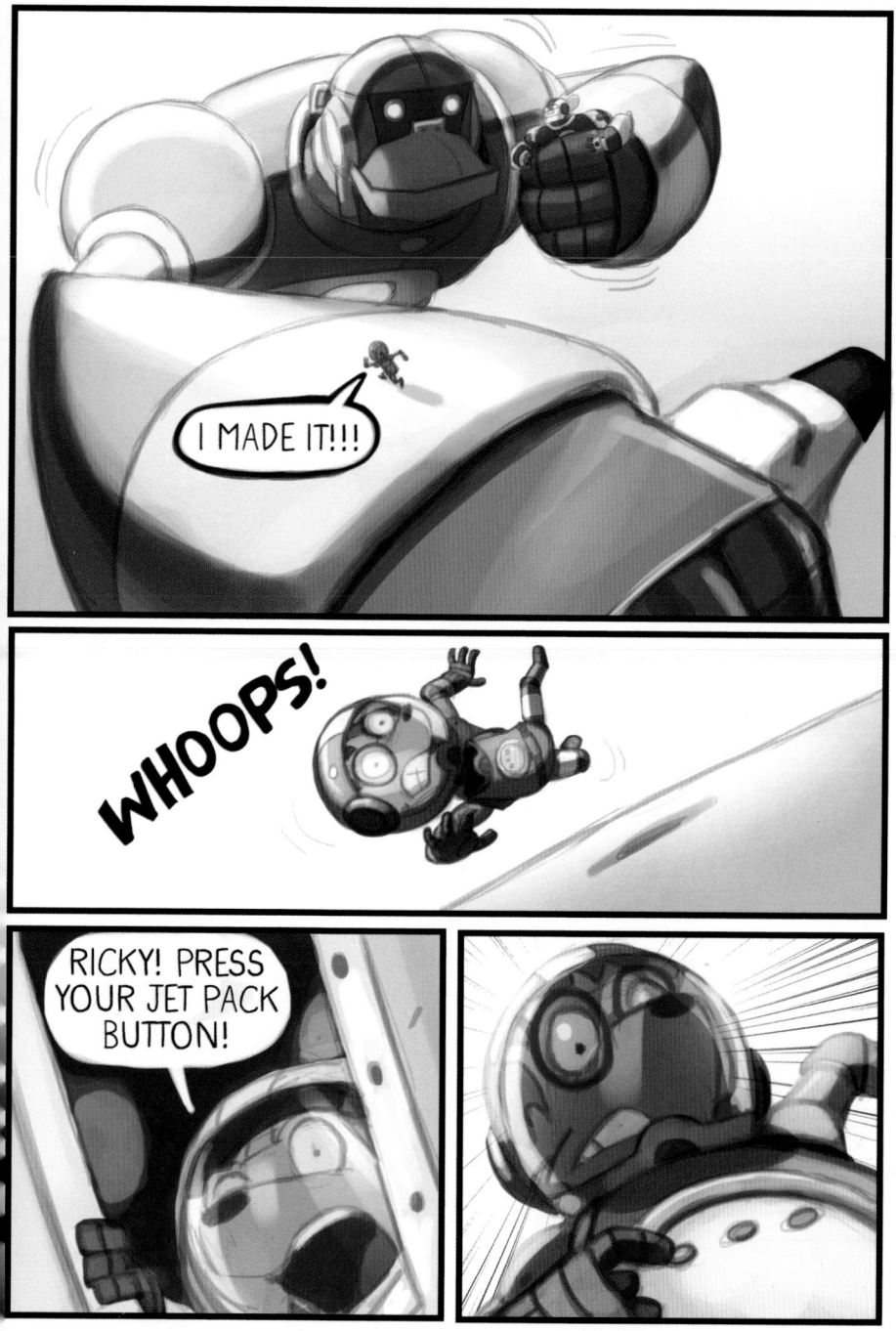
I MADE IT!!!
WHOOPS!
RICKY! PRESS YOUR JET PACK BUTTON!

CLICK
EMERGENCY LIFE RAFT
JET PACK
FLOOD LIGHT
FSSSSSSSSSSS
SSSSSSSSSSSSSSSS
OH NO!
I ACCIDENTALLY PRESSED THE LIFE RAFT BUTTON!

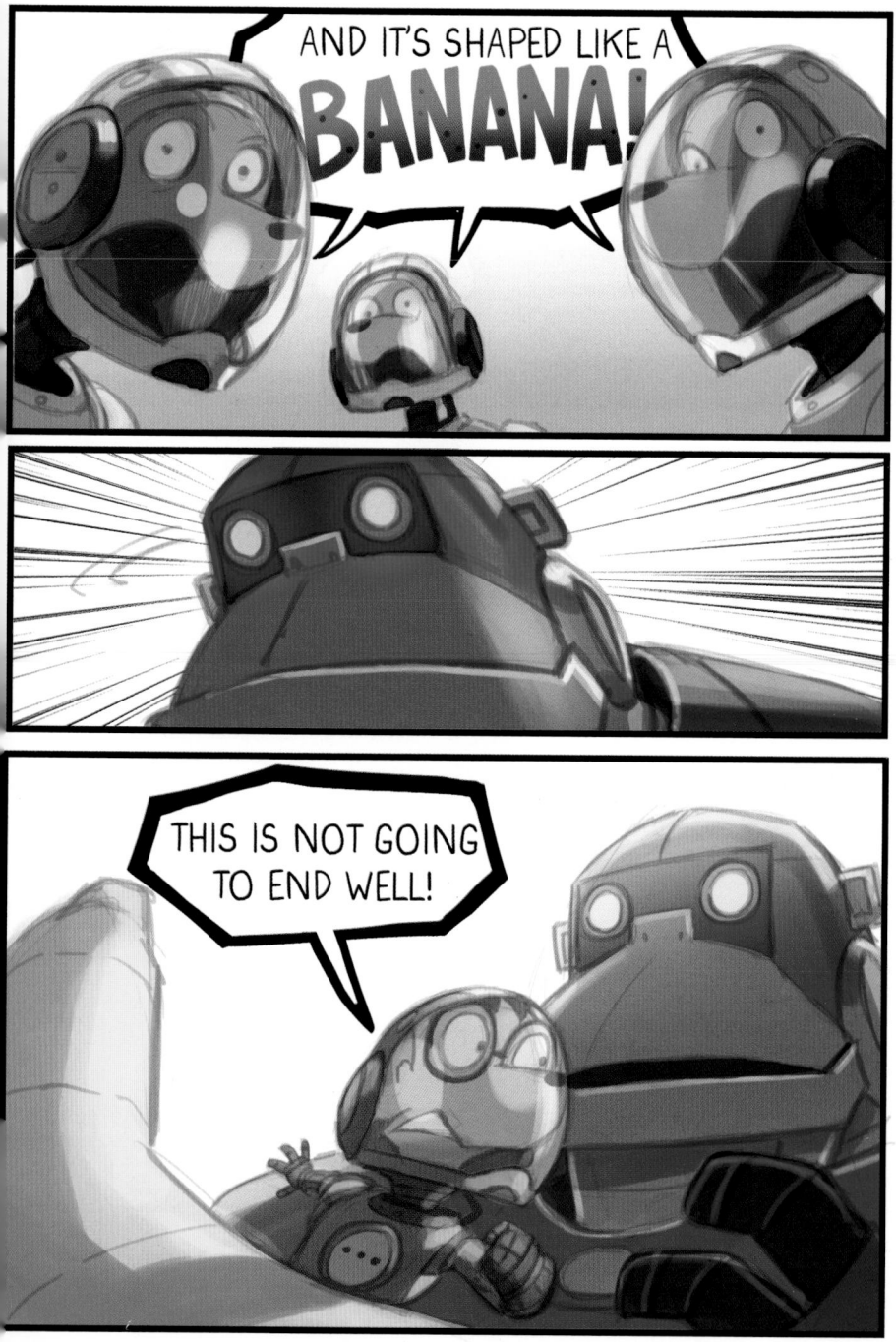
AND IT'S SHAPED LIKE A BANANA!
THIS IS NOT GOING TO END WELL!

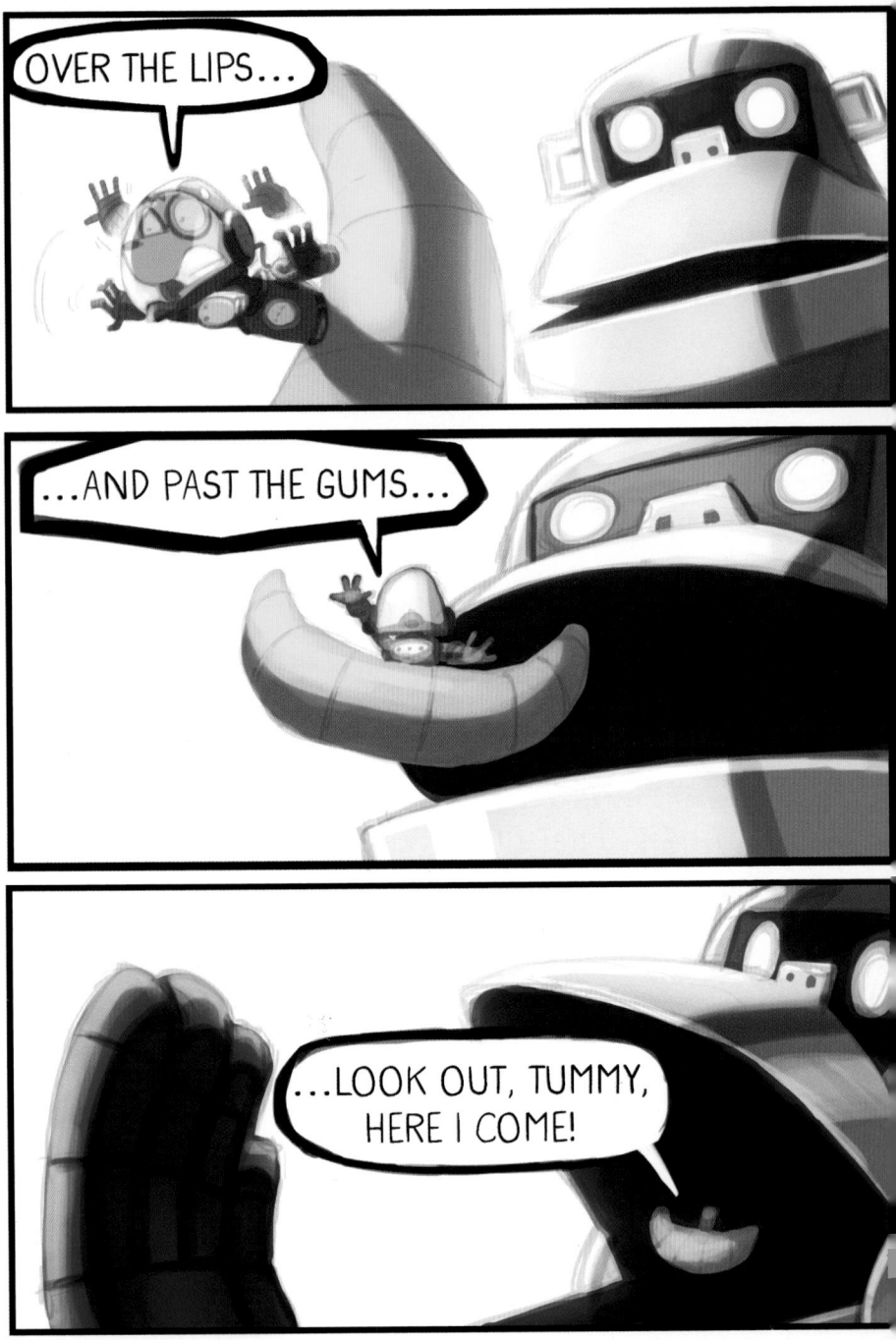
OVER THE LIPS...
...AND PAST THE GUMS...
...LOOK OUT, TUMMY, HERE I COME!

NOoOoOoOo..
WAIT!
YAAAAAA!

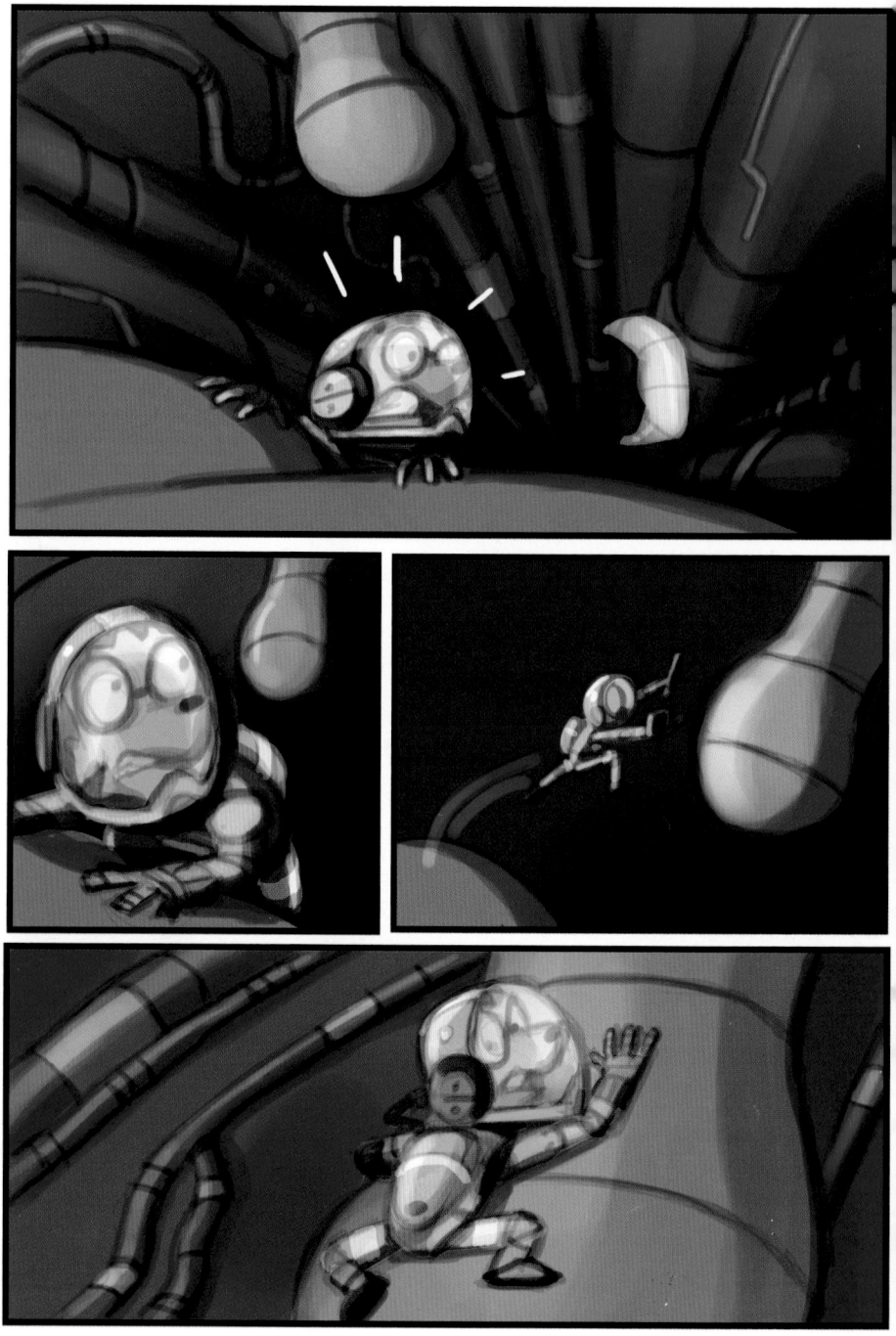

EXIT
EXIT

CHAPTER NINE
RICKY TO THE RESCUE

Ricky had found his way into a strange control center. He looked around nervously. He saw lots of evil robots and many strange machines.

Then Ricky found the main power switch.

Ricky grabbed the switch and tried to turn off the power, but the switch was stuck. Ricky pulled and pulled on the switch.

Finally, Ricky was spotted by an evil Robo-Chimp.

"Destroy the intruder!" said the Robo-Chimp. "Destroy the intruder!"

The Robo-Chimp grabbed Ricky's breathing tube and started pulling. Soon, other Robo-Chimps joined in. Harder and harder they pulled.

Then Ricky got an idea. He wrapped his breathing tube around the main power switch and held on tight. The Robo-Chimps pulled and pulled. Finally, the switch began to move.

The harder the Robo-Chimps pulled, the more the switch moved.

Ka-KLANK!

Suddenly, the power for the whole laboratory turned off.

"Hooray!" cried Ricky.

CHAPTER TEN
FREEDOM

Outside, the Orangu-Tron lost all of its power. Ricky's Mighty Robot pushed his way out of the giant metal hand. He was free at last!

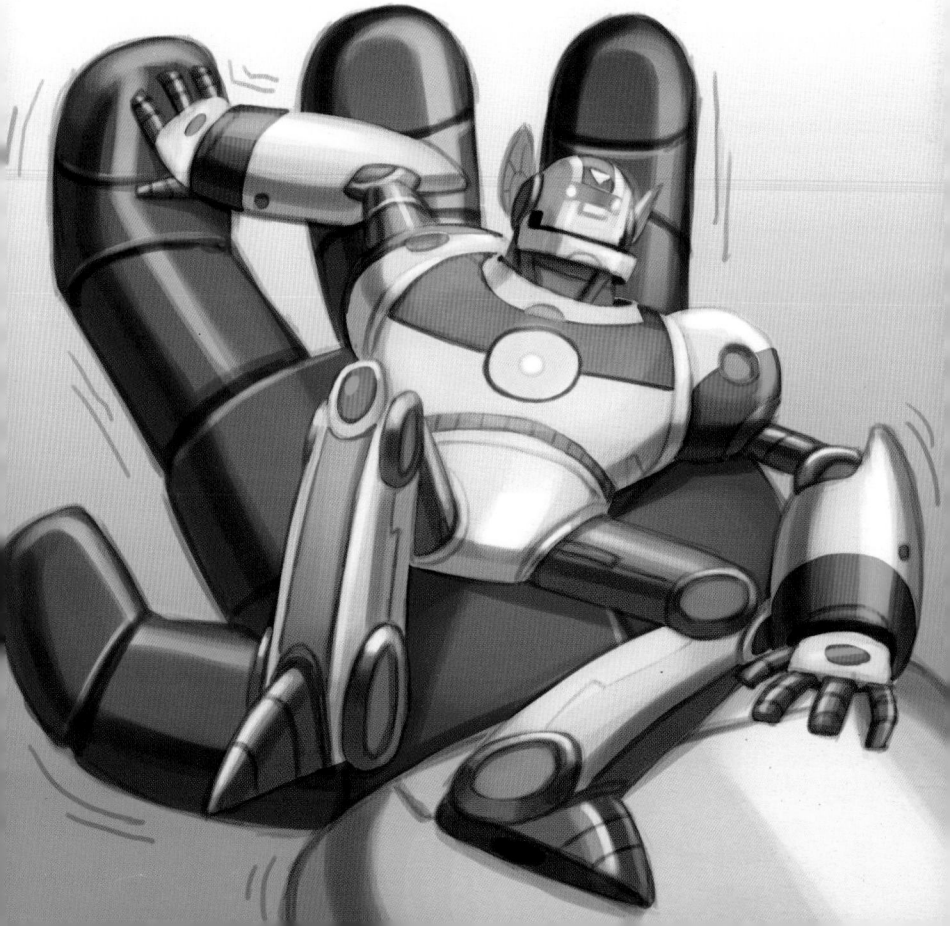

But inside, Ricky was in trouble. The Robo-Chimps rushed toward Ricky. "Must destroy intruder!" they chanted. "Must restore power!"

"HELP ME!" screamed Ricky as the Robo-Chimps came closer and closer.

KER-POW!

Ricky's Mighty Robot punched a hole in the roof and grabbed Ricky just in time.

Ricky pushed the SELF-DESTRUCT button. "Let's get out of here!" cried Ricky as the laboratory began to shake and crumble.

With Ricky in one hand and the space shuttle in the other, Ricky's Mighty Robot zoomed into space – just in time.

KA-BOOOOOOOOM!

"That takes care of Mars," said Ricky. "Now we have to save Earth!"

CHAPTER ELEVEN
BACK TO EARTH

When they got back to Earth, Ricky's Mighty Robot spotted Major Monkey.

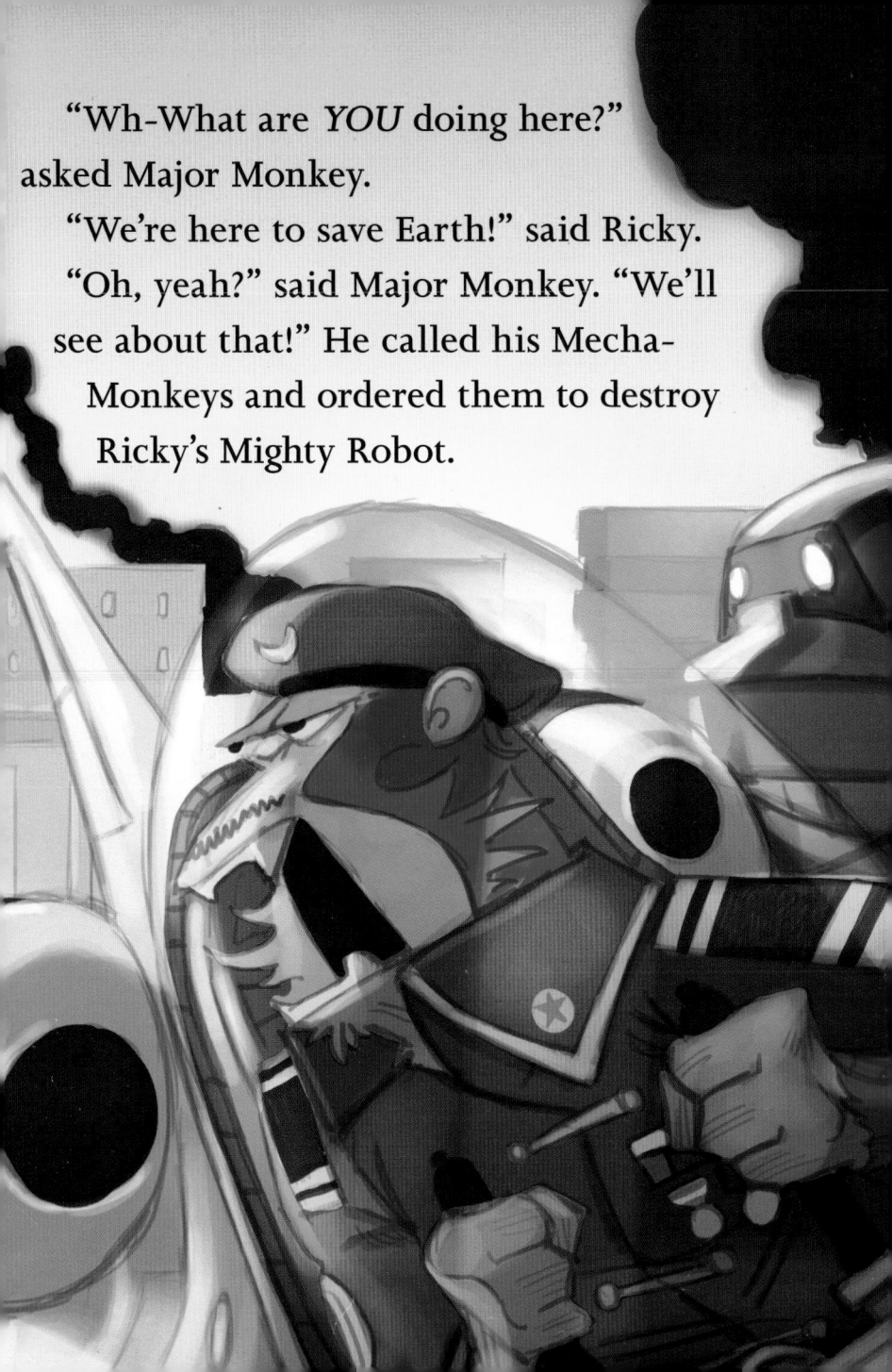

"Wh-What are *YOU* doing here?" asked Major Monkey.

"We're here to save Earth!" said Ricky.

"Oh, yeah?" said Major Monkey. "We'll see about that!" He called his Mecha-Monkeys and ordered them to destroy Ricky's Mighty Robot.

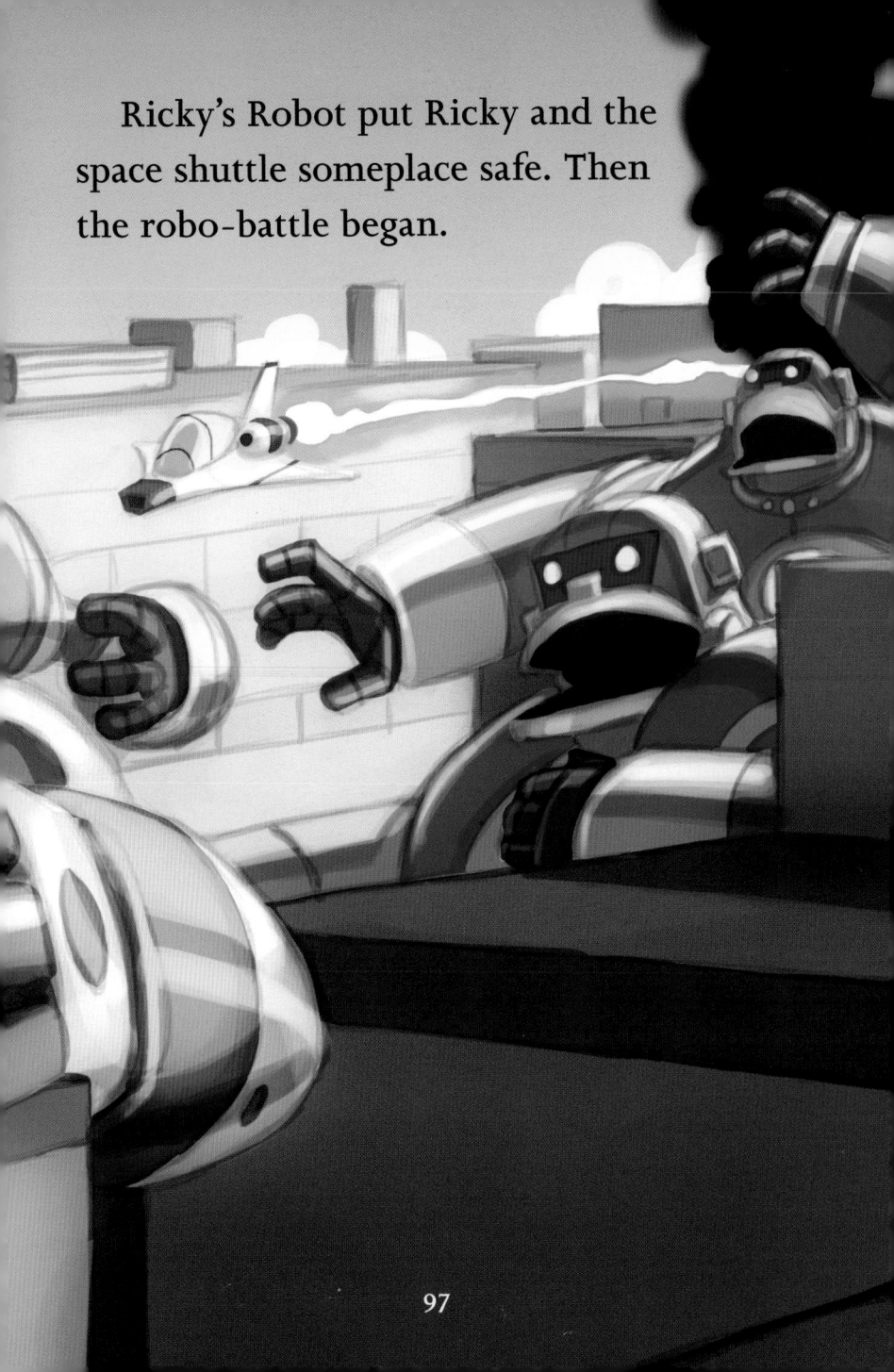

Ricky's Robot put Ricky and the space shuttle someplace safe. Then the robo-battle began.

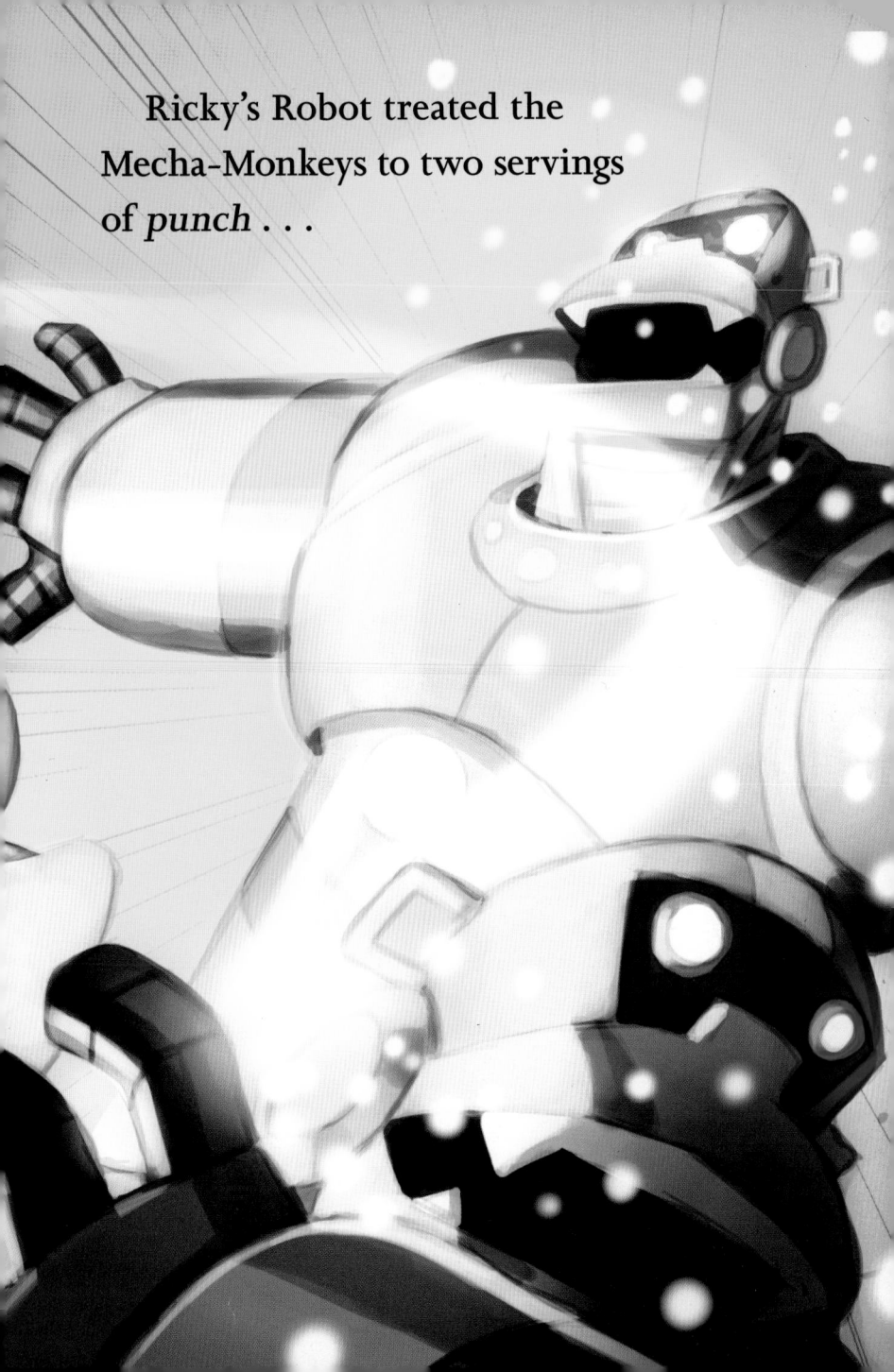

Ricky's Robot treated the Mecha-Monkeys to two servings of *punch* . . .

. . . one *foot-long* . . .

. . . and a *knuckle sandwich.*

Major Monkey was very upset. "All right, banana brains," he shouted. "Quit monkeying around! Let's see some action!"

CHAPTER TWELVE
THE BIG BATTLE
(IN FLIP-O-RAMA™)

FLIP-O
HEY, KIDS! YOU CAN ANIMATE THE ACTION BY FOLLOWING THESE EASY STEPS!

-RAMA

HERE'S HOW IT WORKS!

STEP 1

Place your *left* hand inside the dotted lines marked "LEFT HAND HERE." Hold the book open *flat*.

STEP 2

Grasp the *right-hand* page with your right thumb and index finger (inside the dotted lines marked "RIGHT THUMB HERE").

STEP 3

Now *quickly* flip the right-hand page back and forth until the picture appears to be *animated*.

(For extra fun, try adding your own sound-effects!)

FLIP-O-RAMA 1

(pages 109 and 111)

Remember, flip *only* page 109.
While you are flipping, be sure you
can see the picture on page 109
and the one on page 111.
If you flip quickly, the two
pictures will start to look like
one *animated* picture.

Don't forget to add
your own sound-effects!

LEFT HAND HERE

THE MECHA-MONKEYS ATTACKED.

RIGHT THUMB HERE

RIGHT
INDEX
FINGER
HERE

THE MECHA-MONKEYS ATTACKED.

FLIP-O-RAMA 2

(pages 113 and 115)

Remember, flip *only* page 113.
While you are flipping, be sure you
can see the picture on page 113
and the one on page 115.
If you flip quickly, the two
pictures will start to look like
one *animated* picture.

Don't forget to add
your own sound-effects!

LEFT HAND HERE

RICKY'S ROBOT FOUGHT BACK.

RIGHT THUMB HERE

RIGHT
INDEX
FINGER
HERE

RICKY'S ROBOT FOUGHT BACK.

FLIP-O-RAMA 3

(pages 117 and 119)

Remember, flip *only* page 117.
While you are flipping, be sure you
can see the picture on page 117
and the one on page 119.
If you flip quickly, the two
pictures will start to look like
one *animated* picture.

Don't forget to add
your own sound-effects!

LEFT HAND HERE

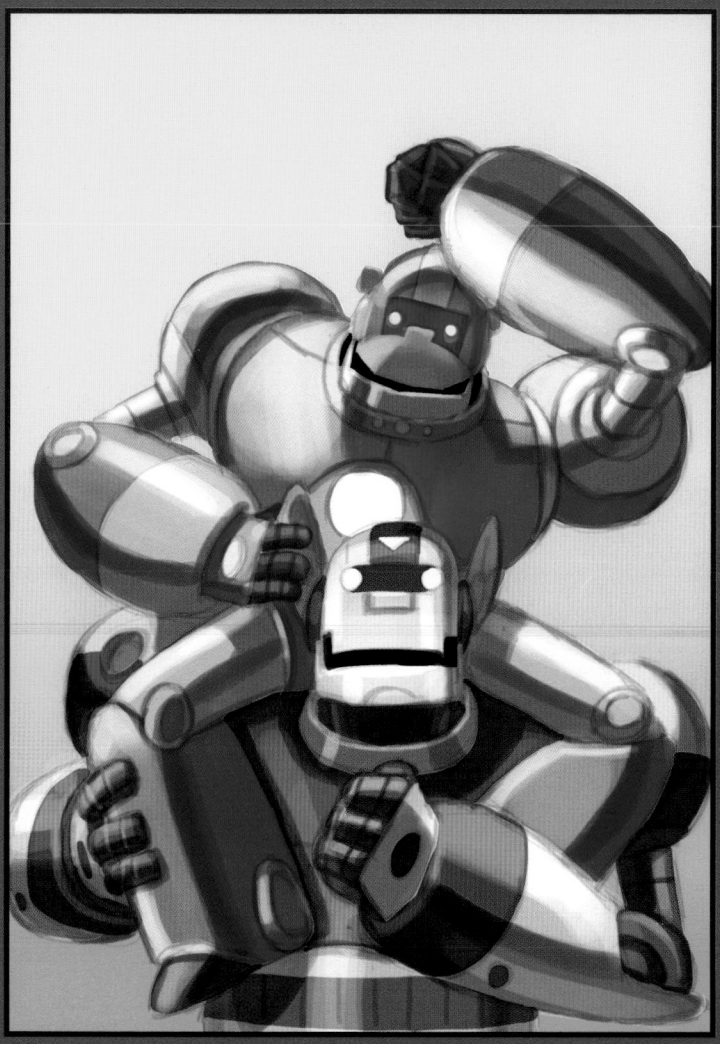

THE MECHA-MONKEYS BATTLED HARD.

RIGHT THUMB HERE

RIGHT
INDEX
FINGER
HERE

THE MECHA-MONKEYS BATTLED HARD.

FLIP-O-RAMA 4

(pages 121 and 123)

Remember, flip *only* page 121.
While you are flipping, be sure you
can see the picture on page 121
and the one on page 123.
If you flip quickly, the two
pictures will start to look like
one *animated* picture.

Don't forget to add
your own sound-effects!

LEFT HAND HERE

RICKY'S ROBOT BATTLED HARDER.

RIGHT THUMB HERE

RIGHT
INDEX
FINGER
HERE

RICKY'S ROBOT BATTLED HARDER.

FLIP-O-RAMA 5

(pages 125 and 127)

Remember, flip *only* page 125.
While you are flipping, be sure you
can see the picture on page 125
and the one on page 127.
If you flip quickly, the two
pictures will start to look like
one *animated* picture.

Don't forget to add
your own sound-effects!

LEFT HAND HERE

RICKY'S ROBOT WON THE WAR.

RIGHT THUMB HERE

RIGHT
INDEX
FINGER
HERE

RICKY'S ROBOT WON THE WAR.

CHAPTER THIRTEEN
PAYING FOR MISTAKES

Poor Major Monkey. His Mecha-Monkeys flew home to Mars, and he could not rule the world anymore.

"Boo-hoo-hoo!" cried Major Monkey. "I've made a big mistake."

"Yes," said Ricky. "And now you must pay for your mistake!"

Together, the two heroes put Major Monkey where he belonged: in the Squeakyville jail.

"Thank you, boys, for saving Earth," said the general. "If there's anything we can do to repay you, please let me know!"

Ricky whispered in his Robot's ear. The Robot nodded his giant head.

"Well, sir," said Ricky, "we sure could use a new minivan."

"All right," said the general. "How many would you like?"

CHAPTER FOURTEEN
HEROES

Ricky and his Mighty Robot flew back to the Space Center to meet Ricky's parents.

"Mom! Dad!" cried Ricky. "Look what the general gave us. A brand-new minivan!"

"Wow!" said Ricky's mother.

"We'll race you home!" said Ricky's father.

So Ricky Ricotta and his Mighty Robot raced the rocket-powered minivan all the way home.

Soon, the whole Ricotta family was safe at home eating cheese pizza and drinking root beer.

"Thank you for rescuing each other today," said Ricky's mother.

"Yes," said Ricky's father, "and thank you for paying for your mistake."

"No problem," said Ricky . . .

. . . "that's what friends are for!"

READY FOR

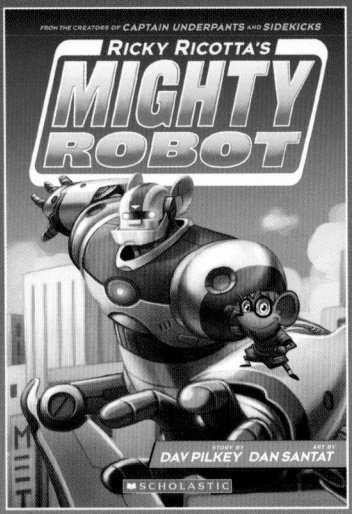
FROM THE CREATORS OF CAPTAIN UNDERPANTS AND SIDEKICKS
RICKY RICOTTA'S
MIGHTY ROBOT
STORY BY DAV PILKEY
ART BY DAN SANTAT
SCHOLASTIC

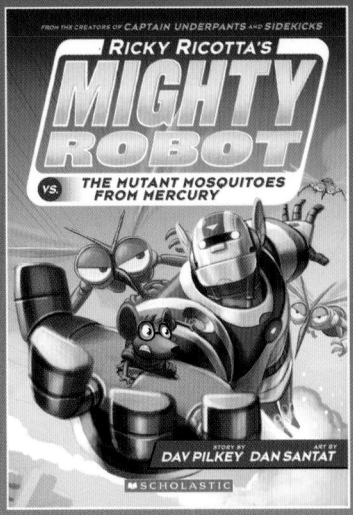
FROM THE CREATORS OF CAPTAIN UNDERPANTS AND SIDEKICKS
RICKY RICOTTA'S
MIGHTY ROBOT
VS. THE MUTANT MOSQUITOES FROM MERCURY
STORY BY DAV PILKEY
ART BY DAN SANTAT
SCHOLASTIC

FROM THE CREATORS OF CAPTAIN UNDERPANTS AND SIDEKICKS
RICKY RICOTTA'S
MIGHTY ROBOT
VS. THE VOODOO VULTURES FROM VENUS
STORY BY DAV PILKEY
ART BY DAN SANTAT
SCHOLASTIC

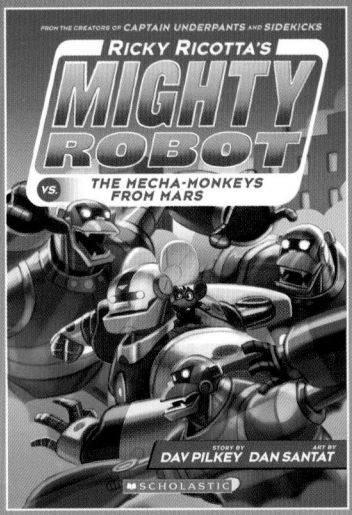
FROM THE CREATORS OF CAPTAIN UNDERPANTS AND SIDEKICKS
RICKY RICOTTA'S
MIGHTY ROBOT
VS. THE MECHA-MONKEYS FROM MARS
STORY BY DAV PILKEY
ART BY DAN SANTAT
SCHOLASTIC

MORE RICKY?

FROM THE CREATORS OF CAPTAIN UNDERPANTS AND SIDEKICKS
RICKY RICOTTA'S
MIGHTY ROBOT
VS. THE JURASSIC JACKRABBITS FROM JUPITER
STORY BY DAV PILKEY
ART BY DAN SANTAT
SCHOLASTIC

FROM THE CREATORS OF CAPTAIN UNDERPANTS AND SIDEKICKS
RICKY RICOTTA'S
MIGHTY ROBOT
VS. THE STUPID STINKBUGS FROM SATURN
STORY BY DAV PILKEY
ART BY DAN SANTAT
SCHOLASTIC

FROM THE CREATORS OF CAPTAIN UNDERPANTS AND SIDEKICKS
RICKY RICOTTA'S
MIGHTY ROBOT
VS. THE URANIUM UNICORNS FROM URANUS
STORY BY DAV PILKEY
ART BY DAN SANTAT
SCHOLASTIC

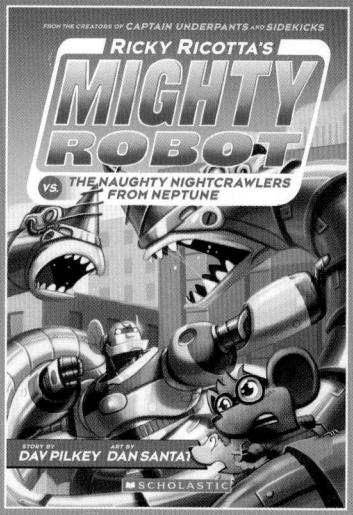
FROM THE CREATORS OF CAPTAIN UNDERPANTS AND SIDEKICKS
RICKY RICOTTA'S
MIGHTY ROBOT
VS. THE NAUGHTY NIGHTCRAWLERS FROM NEPTUNE
STORY BY DAV PILKEY
ART BY DAN SANTAT
SCHOLASTIC

DAV PILKEY

has written and illustrated more than fifty books for children, including *The Paperboy*, a Caldecott Honor book; *Dog Breath: The Horrible Trouble with Hally Tosis*, winner of the California Young Reader Medal; and the IRA Children's Choice Dumb Bunnies series. He is also the creator of the *New York Times* best-selling Captain Underpants books. Dav lives in the Pacific Northwest with his wife. Find him online at www.pilkey.com.

DAN SANTAT

is the writer and illustrator of the picture book *The Adventures of Beekle: The Unimaginary Friend*. He is also the creator of the graphic novel *Sidekicks* and has illustrated many acclaimed picture books, including the *New York Times* bestseller *Because I'm Your Dad* by Ahmet Zappa and *Crankenstein* by Samantha Berger. Dan also created the Disney animated hit *The Replacements*. He lives in Southern California with his family. Find him online at www.dantat.com.